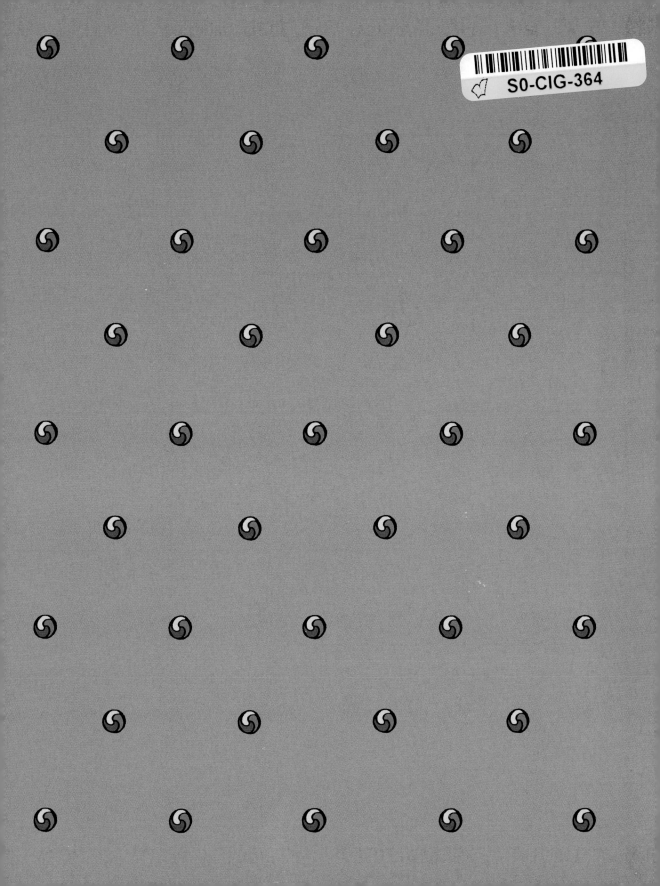

Korean
Children's Day

by Ruth Suyenaga
with Young Sook Kim
and Young Mi Pak

Illustrated by
Nani Kyong-Nan

MULTICULTURAL CELEBRATIONS

MODERN CURRICULUM PRESS

Multicultural Celebrations was created under the auspices of

The Children's Museum, Boston.
Leslie Swartz, Director of Teacher Services,
organized and directed this project with
funding from The Hitachi Foundation.

Design: Gary Fujiwara
Photographs: *10, 13, 14, 17,* The Children's Museum.

MODERN CURRICULUM PRESS, INC.
13900 Prospect Road
Cleveland, Ohio 44136

Published simultaneously in Canada by Globe/Modern Curriculum Press, Toronto.

ISBN 0-8136-2292-1 (soft cover)   0-8136-2293-X (hard cover)

3 4 5 6 7 8 9 10   95 94 93 92

Simon & Schuster   A Paramount Communications Company

My name is Young Soo Newton and this is my best friend, Jeremy Simons.

Jeremy and I are in Mrs. Carnie's champion 4th-grade class at Raymond Elementary School. Champions of what, you might ask. Well, I will tell you the whole story.

First you must realize that we used to be the *only* class that wasn't a champion of something. This story is about how Korean *Children's Day* changed all that.

It all started one day when Jeremy asked, "Young Soo, can you go to the movies with me on Saturday? That new space movie is playing."

2

"I'll ask my mom, but I think she'll say yes. Let's do it," I told him.

When I got home from school, Mom was planting the garden. "I told Jeremy I'd go to the movies on Saturday. Is that okay?"

"Young Soo," Mom said, "have you forgotten that Saturday is May 5th? Your Korean class at the Institute has a special *Children's Day* celebration planned."

She was right—I had forgotten.

5

In Korea, where I was born, *Children's Day* is a big deal for kids. Parents take the day off to visit the museums and parks with their children. All the bus rides are free and neighborhood stores give away candy and balloons.

"Why don't you ask Jeremy to come with us?"

I called him right away. "I forgot that I have to go to Korean class on Saturday."

"I didn't know you took Korean classes. Why? Aren't you already Korean?"

6

I laughed at his questions. "Of course I'm Korean. But since my parents adopted me, I live here in the United States. They just want to make sure I don't forget things about Korea. And tomorrow we're going to celebrate *Children's Day*. Would you like to come along?"

"Wow! You mean Korean kids get their own special holiday? I wish we celebrated *Children's Day* in America. Sure, I'll come."

The next day, when we arrived at the Korean Institute, I introduced Jeremy to Mrs. Kim, the head teacher. Mrs. Kim bowed to us, and Mom and I bowed to Mrs. Kim. Jeremy decided to bow, too.

"That's what people in Korea do when they meet," I told him. "It shows respect."

"Boy, my mom would like that," Jeremy answered.

We walked past a group of kids playing *yut*.

"What are they doing?" Jeremy asked.

"Playing a game with four sticks," Mrs. Kim explained. "They take turns tossing them in the air and moving around the board. You and Young Soo can play later."

"I'd like that. This Institute place is all right! Hey, Young Soo. Can you read that sign?"

10

"Sure," I said. "It's the Korean alphabet, *Hangul*. Those kids are making thank you cards for *Parents' Day* . . . that's on May 8th. I'll show you how to write 'Thank you Mother, thank you Father' in Korean."

"You have a *Parents' Day*, too? Do you have Uncles' and Aunts' days and . . . " Jeremy was full of questions.

It was noon before we knew it. "What's for lunch? Hot dogs?"

"Uh, no. We usually have rice, *kimchi*, *jop chae*, *pulgolgi*, and *mandu*," I told him, a little worried. "I hope you like Korean food."

As we ate the rice, pickled cabbage, noodles, beef, and dumplings, Jeremy said, "This is great. Does your mom make Korean food at home?"

"Yeah—she learned here, at the Korean Institute."

After lunch, everyone sang the *Children's Day* song and three of the older girls performed a dance. "It's a *drum dance*," I told Jeremy before he could ask.

"Now we will have a special *Tae Kwon Do* demonstration," announced Mrs. Kim. "Will Mr. Park's students please get dressed?"

Jeremy was about ready to burst with questions now, but I had to leave him. I put on my white outfit and yellow belt and lined up with the other kids. Then each of us showed our best *Tae Kwon Do* movements.

"Why didn't you tell me you knew how to do judo—I mean *Tae Kwon Do*?" Jeremy asked. "Would you teach me how?"

"I can't. Some people think that you learn *Tae Kwon Do* just to beat people up and break boards. That's the wrong idea. Mr. Park says that studying *Tae Kwon Do* trains your mind and body so you can become strong, patient, and humble. It takes a lot of concentration . . . and practice."

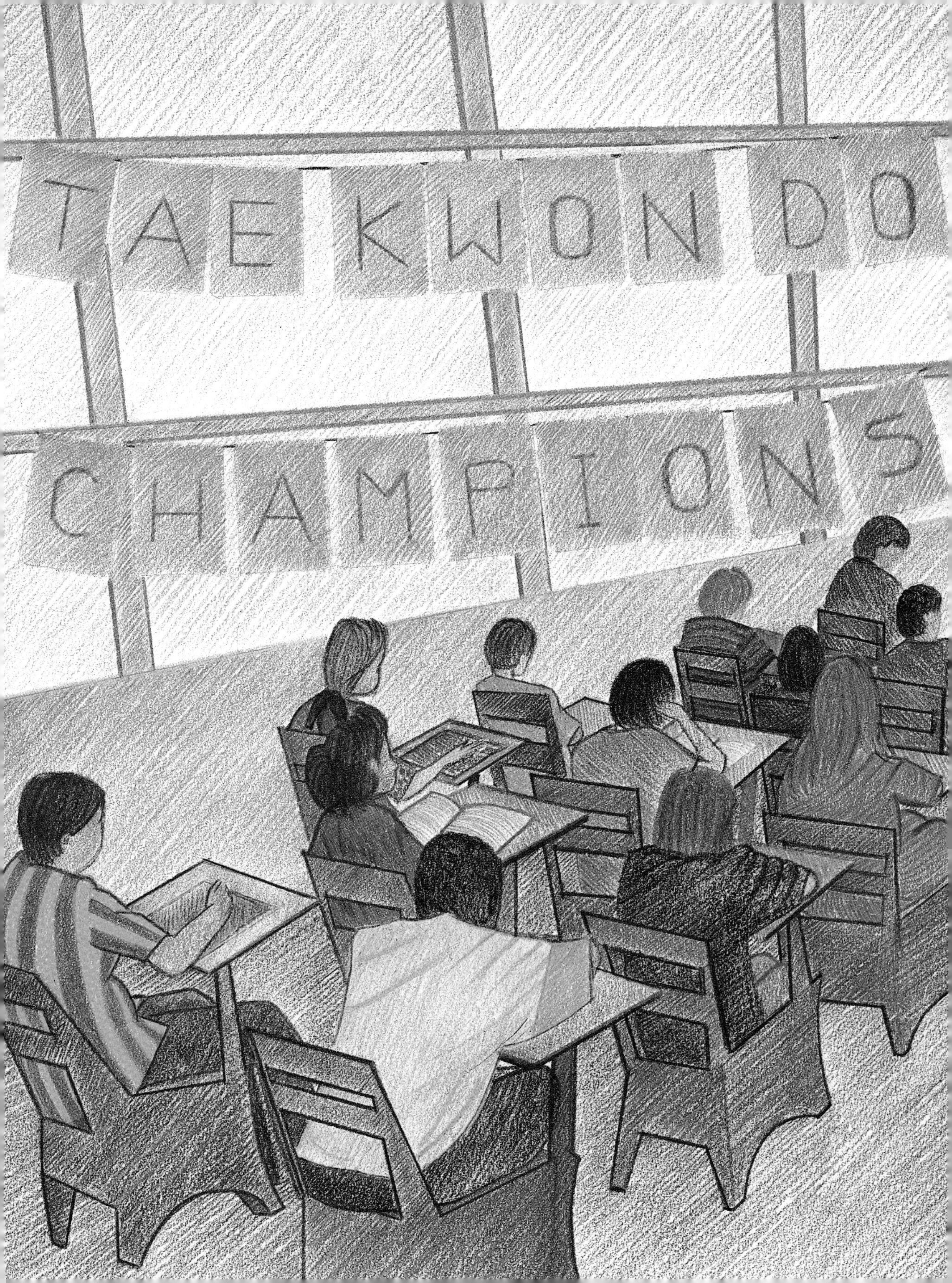
TAEKWONDO
CHAMPIONS

"To learn *Tae Kwon Do*, you would have to take classes like I do. It takes a lot of time, but it's worth it. There are even competitions."

"Well, if all these kids can do it, *I* can do it," Jeremy said. "You know, I'll bet our *whole class* could do it . . . if we had someone to teach us . . . and if we could just convince Mrs. Carnie . . . "

You can guess the rest.

And that's how Mrs. Carnie's 4th-grade class became the *Tae Kwon Do* champions of Raymond Elementary School.

Glossary

Children's Day (CHIL-druns DAY) a Korean holiday for children held on May 5th

drum dance (DRUM DANS) a traditional Korean dance

Hangul (HAHN-gool) Korean alphabet

jop chae (JAHP CHAYE) a popular Korean dish made with transparent noodles and mixed vegetables

kimchi (KIM-chee) pickled cabbage commonly eaten with Korean meals

mandu (MAHN-DOO) Korean dumplings

Parents' Day (PAR-ents DAY) a Korean holiday honoring parents held on May 8th

pulgolgi (bool-GOH-gee) a popular Korean dish made of thinly sliced broiled beef

Tae Kwon Do (TEH KWAHN DOH) Korean martial arts which combine sport, self-defense, and the training of the mind

Young Soo (YUNG SOO) boy's name

yut (YUT) a traditional Korean game played with four wooden sticks

About the Authors

Ruth Suyenaga is a classroom teacher who conducts workshops on Asian Americans and multicultural education. She dedicates this story to her daughter Maile and her son Kenji.

President of the Korean Institute in Cambridge, Massachusetts, **Dr. Young Sook Kim** moved to the United States from Korea in 1980, and earned an Ed.D. degree at Harvard University.

Young Mi Pak grew up in Seoul, Korea, and immigrated to the United States in 1973. She has a M.A. degree in East Asian Studies from Harvard University and is now a doctoral student at Graduate Theological Union in Berkeley, California.

About the Illustrator

Nani Kyong-Nan was born in Inchon, Korea. She came to the United States in 1972, earning a B.A. degree from the University of Hawaii and a M.A. degree from the School of Visual Arts. She works as an illustrator and graphic designer in New York.

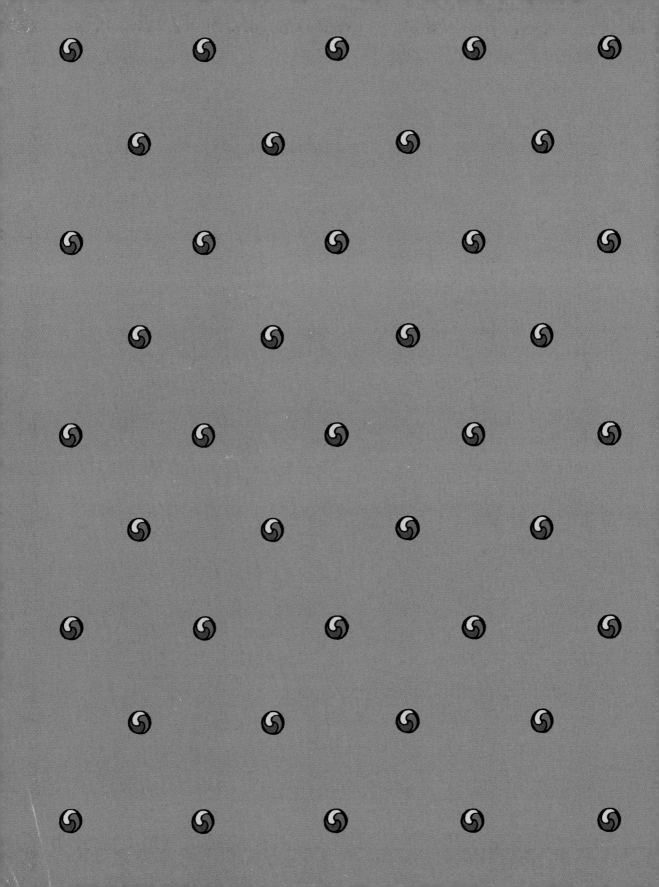